Young Readers Book Club presents...

Charlotte Zolotow

THE POODLE WHO BARKED AT THE WIND

Pictures by June Otani

Harper & Row, Publishers

The Poodle Who Barked at the Wind

Library of Congress Cataloging-in-Publication Data
Zolotow, Charlotte, 1915–
The poodle who barked at the wind.

Summary: A family's noisy little poodle barks at everything, disturbing the father, until the day everyone else goes out and the father and poodle are left alone together.

[1. Dogs—Fiction.] I. Otani, June, ill. II. Title.
PZ7.Z77Po 1987 [E] 86-42992
ISBN 0-06-026965-0
ISBN 0-06-026966-9 (lib. bdg.)

A B C D 0 1 2 3

To Martha and Norman Stein,
with love

Once there was a family with a little black poodle. She was a noisy little poodle and barked at everything.

She barked at the garbage men.

She barked at the postman.

She barked at the milkman.

She barked at the telephone when it rang and the wind when it blew and the rain when it rained.

The children in the family would stop what they were doing to see why the little poodle was barking.

The mother would look up from her work to find out why the little poodle was barking.

But the father of the family was a writer and worked at home. The little poodle's barking made him forget what he wanted to write.

"Oh why do you bark so much!" he would ask the little black poodle. But she would just sit down in front of him wagging her tail against the floor as though he had patted her on the head.

Every time the phone rang, the little poodle barked.

Every time the doorbell rang, the little poodle raced to it barking loudly.

Every time the postman came, the little poodle barked.

The father would come down for his letters and look at the little poodle.

"Why do you bark so much!" he'd say, and the little poodle would sit down in front of him and wag her tail as though the father had patted her on the head.

Sometimes the mother went out.

Sometimes the little boy went out.

Sometimes the little girl went out.

But one day they all went out together.

They left the little poodle's food in her dish and her water in her bowl.

"Take care of her," the children said when they kissed their father good-bye. "She'll be lonely."

"So will I," said the father.

"We'll be back for dinner," the mother said quickly, "and the house will be nice and quiet for you today."

"QUIET!" said the father. "With that poodle here?"

He looked at the poodle, and the little poodle wagged her tail at him. The father climbed upstairs to his study and closed the door with a bang.

He worked at his typewriter all morning.

But the little poodle didn't know the mother and children were coming back for dinner. She didn't understand their all going out together, and now she felt all alone. She couldn't eat her food. She couldn't drink her water.

When the father opened his study door and started downstairs for lunch, he stumbled over something soft that had been pressed up against his door.

It was the little black poodle.

She scrambled to her feet, but she didn't bark.

She walked downstairs with him, rubbing against his ankle as though she were his shadow.

She went under the table while he ate lunch and put her head on his foot.

"Go eat your lunch," the father said. But the little poodle couldn't eat.

The postman brought the mail.

But the little poodle didn't bark.

The milkman brought the milk.

But the little poodle didn't bark.

The wind blew outside, and the little poodle just lay on the father's foot. The telephone rang, and when the father got up to answer it the little poodle trotted along by his side without making a sound.

"Why don't you bark?" the father said. But the little poodle only put her head into the curve of his hand for him to pat her.

The father went back upstairs to work, and like a small black shadow at his ankle went the little poodle, almost as though she were attached to him.

He closed the door to his study, but in a minute he opened it again. He almost tripped over something warm and black pressed against the door.

"What is the matter with you?" asked the father. "Why don't you bark?" It was dark upstairs, and the poodle's eyes shone orange in the light.

"Oh come in then," the father said, and the little poodle came in and went under the father's desk and lay there on his foot.

It was very quiet.

Only the tap tapping of the typewriter filled the room. Outside soft little pats of rain fell against the window, and the wind shook the house. But the little poodle lay there on the father's foot. When the father stopped typing to think, it was absolutely quiet except for the wind and the rain.

The father looked down.

"Why don't you bark?" he asked the poodle, but under the desk the two orange balls of her eyes shone up at him without a sound.

DAD

Late in the afternoon she jumped up suddenly and ran from the desk to the door of the father's study.

Her tail waved back and forth like a black-handled mop.

The father opened the door and the little black poodle raced down the stairs.

Her family was home! The awful feeling of the empty house was gone. She ran back and forth from the mother to the children, barking happily.

She ran to her bowl and swallowed the whole dish of food that had been there all day. She drank her water noisily, and wagging her tail she ran from the windows to the doors barking and barking, though there was nothing outside but the wind.

Upstairs the father heard her and smiled to himself.

She's happy again, he thought. She's taking care of things.

Never again did he say, "Why do you bark so much?" He knew the little poodle's barking meant that his wife and children were in the house, and the little poodle was feeling protective and brave and bold, warning them about bells and people and the rain and the wind.